ESCAPE TO GOMA

ESCAPING THE FUTURE

Vuyo

Ngcakani

Chapter 1

Today is an exciting day. Twelve-year-old Tola Matthews wolfs down his bowl of porridge and dashes out the door to catch the bus to school. He ignores the bang of the wood chair as it falls on the linoleum floor when he jumps up from the table. The din startles his five-year-old sister Lindi and one-year-old sister Nomsa. Normally, his mama wouldn't let him get away with not picking up the chair, but today she lets him run out with a "have a good day!" Little does she know that the day will be anything but.

He doesn't want to be late for school. His Lobani Primary School football team leaves for a tournament in Dembe, a town he had passed through six months ago. It's a warm, sunny April day, and the bus fills with the chatter of excited boys. The team is undefeated in five games, with three wins and two draws. This will be their toughest test yet, and they're looking forward to the challenge.

"Alright, boys," calls Coach Dube. "Everyone is here, so it is time to go. Let's pray for a safe journey and a good game. Tola, can you do the honours, please?"

During his short time at school, Tola has exhibited his love for Jesus and strong prayer life. It is no surprise that Coach asks him to pray, and Tola is happy to oblige. He stands up to face his teammates who have fallen silent.

"Father, thank you for being with us on this trip. Grant us your favour of a safe journey and a game free of injury and foul play. In Jesus' name, we pray. Amen."

There are three adults and fifteen boys on the bus trip.

"How many goals are you going to score, Tola?" asks Vincent Jabavu.

Tola wants to say five but decides on humility. "I'm better at setting them up. I'm going to say one goal and one assist."

"Make sure that assist is to me," says Dumi Kamau.

"I will, but make sure you don't miss."

"I never miss."

That produces a 'we know better' grunt from the other two. Vincent and Dumi are Tola's closest friends. As well as being teammates, they are in the same classes at school. They have made the transition to city life easier, and Tola finds himself missing his village of Dlambona less.

It was six months ago that Tola, his mama, and two sisters had to flee from Dlambona as it was under attack from a rival tribe. His dad, who he called Tata, worked in Lobani as a domestic, so they travelled there to meet him. It was a harrowing journey, one that Tola didn't like to think about.

The Matthews have moved into an apartment building close to the school. It is a modest three-bedroom apartment, with a small kitchen and single bathroom. Mama has done a good job making it a home with donated furnishings and drapes. They still marvel that they don't have to draw water from a well and they don't grow their own vegetables. The store is a short walk away.

Tata still stays with the family that he works for. He comes home on his days off. So the family is together often, which is all Tola ever wanted.

A little over an hour into the journey, the bus comes across an accident on the road between two pickup trucks and a car. All three vehicles have their truck hoods up, and four men are standing around.

"Stay inside, please," says the driver. "I'll go and see what's going on."

Tola moves to the front of the bus. The four men, all about Tata's age, are just standing around, not saying anything. One of them looks up as the bus driver approaches. He has a full black beard and stands a head taller than the others. The men are muscular and one of them has a salt-and-pepper goatee.

Suddenly, all four men point guns at the driver.

"Oh, my god!" Tola shrieks, as he dashes to the rear of the bus.

The other boys crane their necks to see the reason for his panic.

The full-bearded man barks something and the driver lies down on the tarred road. The other three men approach the bus, which is filled with frightened boys, some screaming, and others in silent shock.

"Quiet!" yells the man with the goatee.

"Please, sir," Coach Dube begins, "we are on our way to a football match. These are just..."

The butt of the man's rifle knocks him down. "I said 'quiet!'"

Tola wants to help his coach as his forehead is bleeding but he doesn't move. He sees that a couple of his teammates have tears streaming down their faces though they are stifling their cries.

"My name is Jogba. Everybody out!"

The boys are frozen in their seats.

"Now!"

The other men move through the bus yanking the boys off their seats and shoving them toward the exit and ignoring their shrieks. The driver is thrown back on the bus and the four adults are tied up left on the bus. One of the men takes out a dagger and stabs all the tires rendering them useless.

"What do they want with us?" whispers Dumi.

Tola keeps close to Vincent and Dumi. In Dlambona they learned about gangs raiding villages and taking the young boys to make child soldiers out of them. Vincent and Dumi may not be familiar with the practice. He doesn't want to scare them any further so he says nothing.

They fall behind the pack and are last to exit the bus. The sapphire sky backs up the hot, golden sun which is well on its way to the peak of its journey. The air is still.

"Line up beside the bus and let us look at you," says Jogba. "We need some strong young men to join us in our fight for freedom from tyranny."

He goes down the line, looking at each boy up and down, and feeling their arms as if checking for bone density and muscle mass. Each boy looks away, avoiding eye contact. He comes to Tola last and nods his approval, as Tola looks strong for his age. Tola meets his gaze.

"What is your name?"

"Tola."

"Tola what?"

"Tola Matthews."

Jogba looks Tola up and down again approvingly. Tola shudders.

"We'll take them all," says Jogba to his men.

The men bark orders as they steer the boys onto the trucks. When Tola and his friends are shoved toward the car, Tola notices that it is the Peugeot 504, the same car that he was almost abducted in Nakuru. He looks toward the bus and points to the Peugeot logo hoping someone saw him do so.

Jogba and one of the other men join Tola, Dumi, and Victor in the car. Jogba drives while the other glares, his gun pointed in their direction.

"Where are you taking us?" asks Tola.

They say nothing. Just stare. Tola glances at his chums and sits back in the seat. Even with his heart beating faster than a gazelle attempting to outrun a cheetah, he keeps his wits about him. That's what Tata would want.

They turn off the main road after nine hundred and thirty-three crocodiles. That's how Tata had taught him to measure the length of time. 1-crocodile, 2-crocodile, and so on. They drive through high savannah grassland until they come to a winding, dirt road. That was just a hundred crocodiles.

He stops counting as the dirt road comes through a wooded area which turns into a thick brush. There's no road but the drivers know where they are going. He isn't sure how long they have been driving but it's a long time. Probably a million crocodiles. They drive until they can't drive anymore as the jungle is impassable.

"Get out," says the man with the gun.

They are led through the jungle until they come to a clearing sprinkled with small, mud huts. Teenage boys stop what they're doing and stare at the new arrivals. Tola sees that their eyes are dead and they look emotionless. His blood chills.

"What is this place," asks Dumi.

No one answers him. The three friends join the other boys who are grouped by one of the trucks. Jogba stands on the truck and addresses the newcomers.

"Welcome to The Future," he announces.

Chapter 2

Tola's parents, Jalisa and Thabo, are excited about seeing their son's match. They wait for Vincent's parents to pick them up as they don't have a vehicle.

"This is one thing that I don't like about living in the city," says Thabo. "You have to travel far to see football."

"Not always, Thabs," says Jalisa, affectionately. "Are you having regrets about the move?"

"Yes and no. Somedays I am, and others I'm not. How about you?"

"No regrets at all. I don't care where we are as long as we're all together."

They embrace just as the Jabavus drive up. The men take the front seats while the ladies relax in the back.

"There's a nice restaurant in Dembe that we like to frequent," says Julian Jabavu, or JJ for short. "We'll have time to hit it before the game."

"Fine," Thabo says, quickly. "But it's our treat and we're not taking no for an answer. You guys are driving so the least we can do is feed you."

"Okay, okay, Thabo," says JJ, laughing. "It'll give me a chance to order that steak I avoid because of the price."

He winks at his wife, Khaya, who shakes her head. The exchange is not lost on their friends, and Thabo gives JJ a friendly shoulder punch, which causes JJ to fake losing control of the car.

"How did you come to live in Lobani," asks Khaya. "Vincent has told us a little bit and it sounds like an interesting story."

Thabo leaves it to his wife to tell it.

"Well, Thabo has been working here for about four years, since 1983. About six months ago our village was attacked by the Gamba and we had to escape."

"Oh, my goodness," exclaims Khaya.

Jalisa nods. "It was awful. They set it ablaze as we fled. It is a one-day journey to get to the town of Goma where we caught a bus to Lobani."

"So it was you, Tola, and the girls, travelling alone?" asks Khaya.

"Yes. Tola was a great help. If it wasn't for him, we would have been in serious trouble. He fought off a bandit, climbed a tree to get us food, and helped me carry the baby. He became a man on that journey."

JJ has to brake suddenly as their conversation keeps his focus off the road. The traffic has slowed down and is creeping by a bus surrounded by police cars.

"That looks like the same bus the boys take to their football games," says Thabo. "Wait, isn't that coach Dube?"

"Stop the car!" screams Jalisa.

JJ pulls over and without regard for oncoming traffic, the ladies sprint to where the coaches were chatting with the police. Coach Dube's face falls when he sees them.

"Coach, what is going on?" asks Khaya. "Are the boys on the bus? Are they hurt?"

The police stop them from entering the bus.

"We want to see our sons!" says Jalisa.

"Jalisa, don't tell me that Tola was on that bus."

Jalisa turns to see the familiar face of Officer Kamau. He was the officer who helped them find Tata when they tried to locate him in Lobani.

"Kamau, what is going on?" says Jalisa, not wanting to waste time with small talk.

The officer beckons Coach Dube and gestures his thumb toward the parents, implying that Dube tells them what happened. While the Jabavus fall apart, wailing about the plight of their boy, the Matthews', all things considered, stay calm.

"Think, Coach. Did the men say anything about what they want with the boys?" asks Jalisa.

"No, they didn't. But let's not be naïve. We know that boys are taken and turned into child soldiers for nefarious people."

Khaya Jabavu lets out a shriek as she falls into her husband.

"Look, we have cars out looking for them right now," says Kamau. "The problem is they have a head start and they seem to have disappeared into the grassland. The vehicles they are in are common in these parts."

"If it wasn't for Tola, we would not have noticed the make of the car," says Dube.

"What do you mean," asks Jalisa.

"As he was being led to the car, I saw him point to the car emblem as if it meant something to him."

"What was it," asks Jalisa.

"It was a Peugeot 504."

The Jabavus go home. Khaya is a mess and JJ feels that it would be better if they are at home. Vincent might find a way to give them a call.

"We have to go to Nakuru," says Jalisa.

"Why?" asks Kamau.

Jalisa explains. "After we could the bus in Goma, it started to rain and the roads were slippery. The driver tried to avoid some ostriches crossing the road and lost control of the bus. He managed to regain control but many of us were injured in the accident. We ended up driving to the local hospital in Nakuru. Dr. Mwangi examined us and offered to drive us the rest of the way to Lobani. He was very kind.

"While in Nakuru, Tola was almost abducted by men driving a Peugeot 504. Tola saw the same Peugeot 504 when we stopped in Dembe for a bathroom break. Dr. Mwangi spoke to a man driving that car and his demeanor changed after that. He became unfriendly and distant. We have to find out he knows."

She and Thabo look at Officer Kamau. They don't have a vehicle so he would have to drive them to Nakuru. Through his car's radio, Kamau asks for an update on the search. There have been no positive results.

"Let's go."

Chapter 3

Jogba calls Tola to his hut. It is the only square-shaped dwelling in the compound. All the others are circular. Jogba is seated at a table to the left, with two men carrying machine guns on either side of him. Tola sets his eyes on one of them and recognizes him as one of the men who tried to abduct him in Nakuru. Jogba sees his eyes enlarge.

"I see that you recognize Zoli," he says. "He is the one who told me about you. He was impressed with your skills with a stick. Who taught you Intonga?"

"My Tata," responds Tola, keeping his eyes off Zoli's scowl.

"He taught you well."

Yes, he did, thinks Tola. Intonga is taught to all boys in Dlambona starting at around eight years old. Tata started Tola at five years of age which is why he exceeded his peer group.

"Would you like a drink?" asks Jogba.

He points to a bottle of Chibuku, a beer that Tola is familiar with, as it was something adults enjoyed in Dlambona. Tola used to wonder how people could drink Chibuku as it smelled like dirty socks. He shakes his head to decline.

"What am I doing here, sir?" he asks.

"Sir?! Call me Colonel Jogba, young man."

Jogba steps out from behind his desk and stands in front of Tola. Tola tries not to show it, but his trembling hands and quickened breath show that he is afraid.

"I'm your father now, Tola. I am going to teach you how to be a soldier."

Jogba puts his hand out and Zoli places a gun in it. The colonel takes Tola's hand and lets him feel the pistol.

"It is time to put down the sticks and pick up a gun, Tola. Take it and feel its power."

Tola withdraws his hand quickly, backs up, and runs out of the hut.

"Let him go," he hears Jogba say, laughing.

He sprints to the boy's dwelling which is a large building resembling army barracks. There are ten beds on either side of the building which houses twenty boys. There are two such buildings on the premises. The smaller, round huts belong to the colonel's men, to whom the boys are subservient.

He falls on his bed, face down, and his body shakes as he weeps. The bed is straw, laid down under a coarse blanket. Vincent and Dumi have beds on either side of him.

The boys don't have time to offer consolation as a couple of henchmen storm in.

"Alright, boys, put these on!" one of them orders.

They throw army fatigues at each of the boys. No one moves which is too slow for one of the henchmen. He shoots his gun in the air.

"Now!"

Tola is the first to wear his new attire. Vincent and Dumi follow his lead and soon all the boys have their clothes on.

"Good. Outside you will find boots for each of you. Put them on and line up in the clearing. Run!"

Tola sees that the fatigues fit loosely on many of his friends. Surprisingly his fits well like they were made for him. As he steps outside, he is beckoned by Jogba.

"These are yours," he says. He holds out a pair of shiny footwear. "They are your size."

The other boys are rummaging through a small mountain of boots, looking for matching pairs. Tola hesitates, not wanting to appear as their captor's pet.

"Take them, Tola. Look, I need someone to be a leader amongst the boys I bring in. As I told you, Zoli was impressed with you. You are a born leader. Take these boots and put them on, please."

He said please, but he isn't being polite. His eyes dare Tola to refuse.

The lineup is inspected and Jogba addresses them.

"Do you know why we are here? We are The Future. Ilanga is our country, and it has been taken over by corrupt individuals. How many of your parents are domestic workers?"

He surveys the group and rests his eyes on Tola, who raises his hand. A few of the others follow.

Jogba nods his acknowledgment. "Do you think that is what they want to do? No one grows up thinking I want to raise someone else's children, clean homes, and wipe dirty noses and bums. But they do it and do you know how much they get paid? Peanuts!"

Tola has no idea how much his parents are paid. Yes, they don't have a car or a fancy house, but he doesn't feel like he lacks anything. His home is full of love and laughter and that is all he needs.

As Jogba waxes on about the state of Ilanga, Tola thinks about escaping. The elders in his village have educated the young people about the horrors of what happens when children are kidnapped. The boys are turned into soldiers and the girls are turned into wives. Once they start drugging and getting them to kill, the brainwashing will have begun. They have to leave tonight.

Chapter 4

The hospital in Nakuru is busy. Jalisa rushes past the reception area to Mwangi's office. He isn't there.

"Is Dr. Mwangi in today?" she asks a nurse.

"No, madam. He called this morning to say he won't be coming in."

The drive to Mwangi's house happens in record time. They block him in as he is backing out of his driveway.

"Let me talk to him, Jalisa," says Officer Kamau.

It falls on deaf ears. Joe steps out to protest being closed in only to be met by an accusing Mom.

Mwangi is surprised to see her.

"Jalisa, what are you doing?" he asks.

"Where is my son," Jalisa starts, her finger poking at the doctor's chest.

"What!" Mwangi is genuinely surprised. "Is Tola missing?"

Officer Kamau shows his credentials. "Mr. Mwangi, can we step into your home and talk, please? Tola has been kidnapped. We believe that you can help us."

"Kidnapped? What makes you think I would have anything to do with that?"

"Because the Peugeot at the hospital and the market in Dembe was seen at the scene," says Jalisa.

Joe looks shaken. "I told you at the time that the Peugeot is common around here, Jalisa."

"Then why do you look unsettled, doctor?" asks Thabo. "Do you have children?"

"No, I don't," says Mwangi.

"When you do you will understand our plight," says Thabo. "Please tell us what you know."

"Let's go inside," says Mwangi.

Zawadi, Mwangi's wife, is surprised by her husband's quick return and the guests he brings with him. He gives her an I'll explain later look, and sits them in the living room.

"What do you know, doctor," repeats Thabo. "We don't have a lot of time."

"I'm sorry, Jalisa," Mwangi begins. "They threatened my family."

Jalisa looks away, unmoved.

"Who?" asks Officer Kamau.

"They call themselves The Future and they are led by a man named Jogba Mwangi. He's my cousin."

"I've heard of them," says Kamau. "They are a new group that wants to overthrow the government and our democracy. They are not as dangerous as Boko Haram but if they are kidnapping boys, they are getting close."

"Where can we find them," says Jalisa, impatiently.

"I don't know," says Mwangi. "They move around from week to week. I've never been to any of their bases. They bring their wounded to me."

"What do you mean?" asks Thabo.

"That's how I'm involved with them. When someone needs medical care, they come to me. I'm their doctor. I have a room in the back where they come for bandages; antibiotics; stitches, or minor surgery."

"Show us," demands the officer.

The room has shelving filled with medical supplies. It also has its own entrance so those who needed care don't come through the main house. There is a bed along one wall and an operating table in the centre of the room.

"Some people come here with bullet wounds," says Mwangi, reading their minds.

Jalisa turns to her husband. "This doesn't help us, Thabo. We need to find our boy. What are we going to do?"

Thabo holds his wife tightly.

"How often do these rebels show up here?" he asks.

Mwangi shrugs. "I have weeks when no one shows up. Then I can have times when I have a busy week. It depends on when they conduct a raid. Who knows?"

Thabo speaks up. "Kamau, we have to station some men here to catch any that show up. In the meantime, reach out to other police services for their assistance. We need their help combing through these grasslands and jungles. Also, contact Ilanga Intelligence. What do they know about The Future? They must have information on places they've set up camp. Maybe they use one camp more than others. Go!"

Kamau is amused. "Except for stationing men here as we have just found out about it, the rest is already being done, Thabo. Thank you for confirming that what I have put in motion is correct. Look, why don't you two go home? You have two other children who would love to see you. Go be with them. I will get an officer to drive you home. Let us do our job."

Jalisa agrees. She is tired and wants to see her daughters. Thabo stays behind. He needs to do something and sitting at home waiting for a phone call doesn't cut it.

"Bring our boy home," Jalisa says, as she climbs into the police car.

Chapter 5

Jogba watches as Zoli puts the boys through some paces. First, they jog for one hour around the camp. Then it was time for school, where they are taught the history of Ilanga from The Future's point of view. It is filled with propaganda, and counter to the history Tola has learned previously.

Though Ilanga was never colonized, it has had problems with tribalism and corruption. His parents never shielded him from the truth of human frailty and the inhumane ways we treat each other. The history of Ilanga is not devoid of it. With its abundant natural resources and mineral deposits, the world with all its greed has come knocking.

But Ilanga has managed to keep democracy intact. Elections are lawful and fair. There has been no coup de tat. There is trust in the judiciary and accountability in government. It is a good country to raise a family.

The Future teaches that Ilanga needs to be rescued. "It is under siege," says Jogba. "You are the liberators. I want you to take your training seriously."

Vincent raises his hand. "Excuse me, Captain? When can we go home?"

Tola grimaces. He is stunned by Vincent's ignorance.

Jogba approaches Vincent and stands close enough that Victor must smell his breath.

"You will address me as Colonel Jogba! And you are home!" he bellows. He turns to address everyone. "Get used to your surroundings, boys. You have enlisted in The Future's Army, also known as TFA. Any attempt to escape with be met with dire consequences. We do not treat deserters lightly." He returns to Vincent's face. "Do I make myself clear?"

"Yes, Colonel Jogba."

"I can't hear you!"

"Yes, Colonel Jogba!"

Tears track down Vincent's cheeks.

"I don't like weak soldiers," says Jogba, sneering. "I think it's time to step into the arena. Zoli!"

Zoli marches the boys a short distance through the jungle to a small clearing. The area was small and had they taken ten more steps, they would have fallen down a ten-foot drop into more jungle. The boys form a circle around the first combatants which are Zoli and Vincent.

"Defend yourself," says Zoli, throwing Victor two sticks.

Victor holds the quivering sticks in front of him. Zoli swings at his legs. He falls hard, screaming.

"Get up," says Zoli, in disgust. He looks at Tola. "Show him."

Dumi and another boy help Victor to the spectators. Tola grabs the sticks and squeezes them, allowing them to become an extension of his arms. His eyes bear through Zoli. He thinks about their first encounter and what could have happened to his mama and sisters had he not been victorious. He prays, then he attacks.

His mistake is that he is emotional. His approach is careless and clumsy. His strikes are telegraphed and easily blocked. Zoli strikes back with a sharp blow to his shoulder and a stinging one to his thigh. *Breathe, and take what he gives you*, he hears Tata's voice.

He looks at his teammates. All eyes are on him. He doesn't want to be a leader. He doesn't want to be the one that the boys look to. He doesn't want Jogba's pronouncement to come true. He isn't a mighty man of valour, as his favourite bible character, Gideon, was called. But it looks like he won't have a choice.

"It looks like city life has dulled your skills," scoffs Zoli.

He charges. He looks as big as a mountain and as slow as a tortoise. Tola blocks every strike and follows it up with two of his own. Block, whack, whack. Block, whack, whack.

Zoli stops attacking and waits for Tola to approach him. Tola obliges. With the sticks held out in front of him like the horns of a gazelle, he swiftly skips toward Zoli, with agility avoids a swing, and with both sticks, slashes Zoli's face, forming parallel tracks from his temple down his cheek. Zoli grunts, grabbing his cheek.

Tola doesn't relent. He uses the fact that Zoli is off-balance to continue his assault. He strikes both ankles, causing Zoli to stumble and fall. Then he puts the sticks together, holding them as one does when readying to swing a bat. Screaming, he starts his swing when a gunshot goes off.

Chapter 6

Mwangi and Zawadi are gracious and cook Thabo and Officer Kamau a delicious meal of umnqusho, peri-peri spiced chicken, and sukuma. The men devour it down not realizing how hungry they are. The meal is chased with ginger beer and coffee.

Around 4 pm, an Intelligence agent Smithson Njoroge comes in and sits at the kitchen table with satellite photos showing part of the boy's journey.

"With the foliage of the jungle, we are unable to see exactly where they went. But we have an idea because we know of two roads in and out of the area. They may have parked and taken off on foot, we don't know. Jogba is not a dumb man."

"Have you dealt with him before?" asks Thabo.

"I haven't personally," Njoroge responds. "But we have a dossier on him. He has upped his game, that's for sure."

"When do we move out?" asks Kamau.

Njoroge closes his file. "I came as a courtesy, Officer. We have taken over this investigation and have our people, who have been trained in tracking and apprehending terrorists, on the job. Thank you for bringing this to our attention. We'll take it from here."

Njoroge gets up to leave. Kamau blocks his path.

"This is my case until I hear from my superiors," he says.

"You're welcome to give them a call," says Njoroge. "Nothing will change."

"Can I use your phone?" he asks.

Mwangi directs him to the kitchen. Njoroge is right. No amount of protesting alters that the police department is out and the Intelligence Service is in.

Kamau can't bring himself to say anything. He paces up and down, scratching his head and gritting his teeth.

"How many men can you get to go find my son?" Thabo asks.

Kamau glares at him. "Are you making fun of me? You heard Njoroge, right?"

"Kamau, I know that area that was on that satellite image. It is an area I frequented with my father when I was a boy. I have an idea where Tola is. That is unless they have moved on. If they have, they haven't gone far. But we have to move now."

"There's no way my superiors will sanction any rescue attempt. Not after Intelligence has taken over."

"I guess I'm on my own then," said Thabo, putting on his jacket.

"What are you doing? You don't have a car."

"No, I don't."

They stand there looking at each other. Kamau doesn't like the idea of the two of them attempting a rescue. No one knows how many men they would be going up against. He asks to use the phone again.

"Hello, Grace."

Grace works at Intelligence as an executive secretary. She went through the police academy with Kamau but after a year of policing, Grace decided it wasn't for her.

"What do you want now, Kamau? You've got to stop calling me here."

"You know you like it when I call," says Kamau, smiling. "How are you, my dear."

"I am well, old friend," replies Grace. "How are you?"

"Not as good, I'm afraid. We have a situation and I need your help. Do you know an agent named Njoroge?"

Grace grunts. "I've met him. He is a good agent but he thinks more highly of himself than he should."

"Some boys have been kidnapped by The Future and we're…"

"That's your case," interrupts Grace. "How can I help?"

"Well, Njoroge was here and Intelligence has taken over the case. We have an idea where the boys are but Njoroge won't tell us what their plans are. The parents of one of the boys are good friends of mine so I have a vested interest in being part of the rescue. Can you find out what Intelligence intends to do?"

"Give me an hour. Where can I call you?"

They don't have to wait long as Mwangi's home phone rings twenty minutes later. Grace informs them that Intelligence will be raiding the camp in a few days.

"In a few days?" Kamau growls. "Don't they realize that they could move on by then? They don't stay in one place for too long."

"Yes, they know that, Kamau," says Grace, gently. "They feel that because they are unsure about the location now, it makes little difference if they move in a few days. They will keep an eye on the satellite images to see if there's any movement."

"Those Intelligence people have no intelligence at all," says Kamau, frustrated. "Thank you for your help, my friend."

Kamau hangs up and informs Thabo of the news.

"Well, what are we going to do officer?" asks Thabo. "Am I going home to tell my wife to wait a few days, or are we going to rescue some boys?"

"Do you know how to use a gun, Thabo?" asks Kamau.

Thabo shakes his head.

"Do you know how much firepower Jogba has at his camp?"

Thabo shrugs.

"I don't either. But I'll bet it's a lot. A couple of guys with some pistols isn't going to cut it."

Thabo says nothing.

"We'll go, but it is a scouting mission. Once we know where they are we will leave and return with reinforcements. Is that understood?"

Thabo nods.

"Let's go and find a LandRover."

Chapter 7

"How much longer?" asks Officer Bulelo.

Kamau had recruited him for extra help in case they needed it. At twenty-four years old he was a new graduate of the academy and had graduated top marksman in his class.

Thabo smiles. "You sound like my son."

They have been navigating the jungle for about an hour. The LandRover had been parked and covered with brush at the edge of the jungle and they travelled the rest on foot. Thabo had wisely advised the officers to bring a flask of water and fruit. He also insisted on purchasing a small spray can of luminescent yellow paint to mark trees they pass in the jungle.

"You'll never find your way out if you get lost," he said, spookily.

It's early evening. The sun has dropped, exposing a bright moon and a multitude of bright stars, and a breeze cools the air. Thabo raises his fist, using the sign for 'stop' that he has seen in the movies. He gestures with his head indicating to the left. About a hundred feet down is a couple of armed teens.

"We must be close," says Thabo.

Kamau agrees. "The young men are probably the outer guards. I wouldn't be surprised if we still have a fifteen-minute hike to reach the camp." He looks around. "I don't see anyone else around."

He looks at the two boys.

"Bulelo, you're with me. We're going to question those boys. Thabo, stay here."

The officers disappear into the jungle. Soon Thabo can't hear them as they approach the boys. He looks toward them looking to see the officers apprehend them. He didn't have to wait long. One minute the boys were there. The next they weren't. Officer Kamau beckoned Thabo.

"That was impressive," says Thabo.

The teens sit down with their hands cuffed behind them.

"What?" asks Bulelo. "Two grown men taking down two small boys impresses you?"

"Well, when you put it like that, I guess not."

Bulelo and Kamau share a smile. They turn their attention to Jogba's guards.

"What are your names?"

"Thomas."

"Sipho."

"Okay, Thomas and Sipho. You are not in any trouble. But you have to help us."

Thomas won't meet their eyes. Sipho is braver.

"Help you do what?" he asks, somewhat defiantly.

"You boys are with The Future, right?" asks Bulelo.

Sipho shrugs and says nothing.

"Where is Jogba Mwangi?"

The two boys shake their heads. "We can't tell you anything," says Sipho. "Jogba said he would hurt our families if we did anything that would jeopardize his plans. We can't even try to run."

"That's right," says Thomas, his eyes filled with fright. "We saw what he did to the father of one of the soldiers when he tried to run. He made us watch as a warning. It worked."

"Just tell us where and how far the camp is," says Kamau.

The boys remain silent. Thabo steps forward.

"My son was kidnapped today. Do you know if he's safe? His name is Tola."

Thomas and Sipho perk up. "Tola is your son," says Thomas. "Wow!"

The men look at each other, intrigued.

"He is fantastic at Intonga," says Sipho. "He beat one of Jogba's henchmen pretty badly."

The boys laugh.

"What happened," asks Thabo, concerned. "Was he punished? Did they hurt him?"

"Hurt him?" scoffs Sipho. "He is Jogba's prized recruit. He likes him. I think Jogba has big plans for him. No one is going to hurt him."

Thabo isn't relieved. He grabs Thomas' scruff.

"You tell me where he is right now."

Thabo's screech sends some birds to flight.

"It is twenty minutes in that direction," Thomas says, pointing. "But you never heard it from us."

Chapter 8

Tola, Dumi, and Vincent sit on the dirt ground in front of their hut. After supper, they are allowed to hang out until bedtime.

Tola isn't saying much. He is shocked at the realization of what he is capable of. He was going to kill Zoli had Jogba not shot his gun off. Zoli was going to bear the full brunt of his anger and frustration caused by where they found themselves today.

He misses Dlambona. It wasn't perfect but it was home. Mama and Tata are trying to make a good life for them in Lobani but he thinks they miss the simple life of Dlambona too. The fateful night when the Gamba tribe attacked changed their lives forever.

"We're out of here tonight," he announces.

Vincent looks incredulous. "Right! We're going to traipse through the jungle in the dead of night and be home by daybreak," he says, sarcastically. "Don't be ridiculous."

"Well, I'm leaving. You can come with me or stay here hoping to be rescued."

"Are you serious? You have no idea what's out there at night. Look, Tola, I know you lived in a village. You come from places like this and we don't. But leaving here at night is reckless. Do you think that your parents would want you to do that?"

Tola hesitates. They left Dlambona in the dead of night but that was mostly grassland and desert. He had traveled to jungle areas with some of the men of the village when they went on school trips. He does not doubt that his parents would want him to leave if he is in danger and they certainly are in danger of being part of The Future.

"Besides, from what you told us about your parents, don't you think that they are trying to rescue us?" asks Dumi.

Dumi has a point, thinks Tola. It is unlikely that his parents are sitting around doing nothing. But they wouldn't want him doing that either.

"Yes, I am serious." His voice drops to a whisper. "Did you see the empty look in the eyes of the guys when we arrived? They have been drugged. Do you want to end up like them? If we stay here longer, we will. We have to leave tonight."

"What do you think, Dumi?" asks Vincent.

Dumi looks at Tola. "Can you teach me Intonga?"

Tola is surprised. He would have expected that request to come from Vincent. Dumi is more of a thinker than a fighter.

"Absolutely, Dumi," he says.

Tola remembers the first time he picked up the two sticks and how he clumsily held and swung them. Through patience and daily repetition, Tata had taught him the skills to become proficient. It got to the point where he was so much better than his peers that he would enter competitions for older teens and win.

But he had never taught anyone. Vincent and Dumi are both athletic and would probably pick up the basics quickly. But becoming skilled takes time. The jungle is full of suitable sticks. After fashioning a few into the appropriate length and removing leaves and twigs, Tola put his friends through the basics.

Bedtime is whenever Jogba says it is. Tonight it is around 9:30 when the rhino horn is blown, which means that around 9:40, the henchmen will come around to ensure that everyone is compliant. True to form, they come around, poking or whacking beds with sticks to ensure there are bodies in them, and laughing at the grunts or yelps of pain. Twenty minutes after that, the three boys run into the forest.

Chapter 9

Thabo, Kamau, and Bulelo see the camp from their vantage point. After letting Sipho and Thomas go, believing that they wouldn't double back to warn Jogba, they navigated the jungle for about 30 minutes to their current position. They never ran into more guards which they found odd.

"Jogba's arrogance will be his undoing," says Kamau.

"Now what?" asks Thabo.

"We agreed that this would be a scouting mission," says Kamau. "So now we know where they are, we will leave to get reinforcements. Let's go."

The officers turn to leave.

"I'm staying," says Thabo.

"Thabo, we agreed," says Kamau.

"I know but hear me out. What if they move before you have a chance to return? I can mark the route they take with something easy to follow."

He shows them the luminescent yellow paint.

"Okay," says Kamau. "But stay out of sight. We don't need another kidnapping on our hands."

Thabo watches them leave and then turns his attention to the compound. Boys mill around the camp but there is no sign of Tola. There is no sign of the football team. He is thankful that they ran into the two guards because they assure him that Tola is here.

Thabo hears the sound of the rhino horn going off and then sees the camp clear as the boys make their way to their huts. He surveys his surroundings and finds two suitable sticks. After removing the bark, he swings them around like he was battling intonga with his shadow. Then in true Matthews tradition, he sprays a twig with the paint and inscribes 'Tola' on one stick and 'Nomsa & Lindi' on the other.

Sipho had mentioned that Tola's dwelling was toward the back of the camp. To his left he sees a couple of armed boys so he makes his way right, keeping under cover heavy brush. Thankful for the bright night, the huts are in full view. As he looks to make a comfortable place to wait for the arrival of the reinforcements, he sees the three boys dash out of one of the huts and into the jungle. Resisting the urge to call out, he chases after them.

Chapter 10

"Keep running," Tola pushes.

They stay off manmade paths and stick to being hidden in the forest. Even though it would slow them down, it feels safer as it would also slow down any pursuers. Being agile and athletic, they can move pretty quickly, bounding small bushes with ease and swiftly rounding trees where they can. Each of them has two sticks which they use to whack brush aside. Tola has the lead.

He is running again. Some months ago he was running for his life with his Mama and sisters. It was a frightening experience but he learned a lot about himself. He learned that he was capable of defending himself and others; he learned that he had courage and strength beyond his years; he learned how to take charge of situations, and he learned that there is no driving force stronger than that of love of family.

This is what drives him tonight. He will not be a statistic of a lost or dead boy soldier. And neither will his friends. He knows that he will be back for his other teammates but taking them all at this time would be foolhardy.

"Tola!"

Tola isn't sure that he hears his name. He keeps running.

"Tola!"

It's a little louder this time so he looks behind him but sees nothing. *Is Jesus calling me?*

"Do you hear someone calling your name?" asks Vincent.

"Yes," answers Tola. "Don't stop. It could be one of Jogba's men."

The sound of a chaser increases. The distant rustle becomes louder, increasing to someone crashing through the brush.

"Find a place to hide, guys," says Tola. "It looks like we may have to fight."

Tola takes a position behind a tree and readies his weapons. *Lord, as David slew Goliath, may we be victorious today.* He takes deep breaths to slow his breathing. He can't see Dumi and Vincent but they must be freaking out. *This morning we were going to play a football game. Now we're running for our lives and may have to fight to prevail.*

He is so focused on breathing that he doesn't hear the silence of the forest. There is no call of his name nor the sound of chasing feet. He peeks around the tree in anticipation of someone appearing through the thicket.

Silence.

The boys emerge from their hiding spots.

"What happened?" asks Dumi.

Vincent shrugs. "I don't know but let's keep moving."

Tola's curiousity gets the better of him. He needs to solve the mystery so he approaches the area of the disappearance.

"Tola, let's go," Vincent insists.

Tola doesn't comply. "I'll be quick," he says.

He looks for signs that someone was chasing them. Although the sky is clear, the tree cover blocks the light of the full moon and numerous stars, making it difficult to see much. He turns to head back to his chums and trips over something. It is a stick just like the one used for Intonga. Not seeing anymore, he joins his friends.

"Look what I found," he says. "Someone was definitely here."

"This is scaring me," says Dumi. "We've got to go."

"Okay," says Tola, taking the lead once again.

It is about ten minutes of leaping over bushes, dodging insects, and avoiding tree trunks. There is the occasional glint of wildlife eyes but thankfully none approach or give chase. A community of chimpanzees swing by out of curiousity but seem uninterested in the runners.

Tola stops when they come to a road that is carved through the jungle. A few seconds later Vincent and Dumi fall at his feet as they heave to recover from their loping.

Tola laughs. "You city boys have no stamina," he says, shaking his head.

"How are you not panting?" Dumi gasps.

Tola doesn't have time to respond as lights appear in the distance.

"Friend or foe?" asks Vincent.

The lights draw close as they contemplate the question.

"Foe," says Tola, deciding that the risk is too great to guess otherwise.

They scurry back into hiding and watch as a Land Rover passes by. It is difficult to see the occupants. Tola wasn't looking at them anyway. As the headlights neared, they shine on the stick he holds and reveals the names of his sisters left by his Tata.

"We have to go back," he announces.

Chapter 11

Dumi and Vincent stare at their friend.

"You're kidding, right?" asks Vincent. "Have you lost your mind?"

"No," says Tola. "Look at this."

The boys see the names of Tola's sisters.

"We have a tradition in the Matthews family. I'm not sure who started it but I know that my grandfather did this as well as my father did. We inscribe the names of our children on our sticks. The idea is to remind us of the reason we are in battle. Tata says that taking up arms is taking care of your family. Whether your home, village, or country is being attacked, it is your family that you consider as you fight."

"Are you saying that you think it was your dad chasing us?" asked Dumi.

"I'm saying it was my dad chasing us. This Intonga stick has my sisters' names written on it. If Tata had two, my name would be on the other. If Tata has been seized by Jogba's men there is a chance that my name would be noticed."

Dumi places a hand on his friend's shoulder.

"It's more likely that he dropped that stick as well. I wouldn't worry about that. But what are you thinking? Are we going to mount some kind of rescue?"

"Do you have a plan, Tola?" asks Vincent.

He doesn't. "I'm open to ideas."

An owl swooped by, calling out, sending a shiver down the boys' spine.

"We should go back," says Dumi.

"We are going back," responds Vincent.

"I mean we should go back to our beds as if we never left," Dumi explains. "It will be easier for us to rescue your Dad from the inside than from the outside."

Dumi makes some sense, Tola thinks. The problem is they don't know if it was Jogba's guys that took him. They aren't even sure what happened. One moment Tata was crashing through the forest; the next moment he vanished like smoke.

"Let's go back to where we found this stick and look around," he suggests. "I might have missed something."

The return back to the area was more of a jog than a dash. The occasional flutter of an owl's wings or the scurry of an animal are the only sounds heard. The boys say nothing.

"Spread out a bit," says Tola, "but don't go far. We don't need another disappearance."

"Do you think anyone at the camp has noticed that we're gone?" asks Dumi.

Tola doesn't get a chance to respond as he hears a groaning.

"Did you guys hear that?" he asks.

"Hear what?" asks Vincent.

"Listen," says Tola.

In the stillness, they hear the groan again.

"That came from over here," says Tola, moving toward a huge baobab tree.

"Hello!" someone shouts.

"Hello," Tola responds.

"Is that you, Tola."

"Tata?"

"Be careful, son. I fell into a hole, probably one dug for an animal to fall into. I must have been knocked unconscious when I hit this giant root. Are you boys okay?"

"Yes, Tata. How about you? We heard you groaning."

"I have a massive headache," says Thabo. "Let me see if I can climb out of here."

With the tree canopy blocking the moonlight, Thabo finds it difficult to locate anything to hold onto or to place his hands and feet. The edges are slippery and anything he grasps is brittle and snaps easily against his weight.

"Keep trying, Tata," says Tola. "We'll see if we can find some vines to pull you out. Come on, guys."

Tola remembers swinging from vines in Dlambona. He enjoyed swinging and dropping into the local pond. The kids would compete to see who could swing the highest. That always worried his Mama.

"Will this work?" asks Dumi.

He points to a vine wrapped around a tree trunk.

"That is perfect, Dumi," says Tola. "Help me pull it down."

They yank onto the vine but it resists.

"Pull on three, guys," yells Tola. "One. Two. Three. Pull!"

They repeat the count until the vine gives way causing the friends to fall on each other. Following their laughter, they gather the vine and tie it to a low-hanging branch. Suddenly, a flashlight shines in their direction.

"What do we have here?" asks Zoli.

Chapter 12

Zoli and the salt-and-pepper goatee man approach the boys.

"You boys are supposed to be in bed," says Zoli. "What are you doing here?"

The boys say nothing.

"What are you planning to do with that vine?" asks Zoli. "Are you going to hang yourselves?"

The two men guffaw.

"You wouldn't be the first," Zoli says, ominously. "Now let's go back to the compound. Colonel Jogba will be interested in your expedition."

Dumi starts to move but Tola stops him.

"We're not going back," Tola says, taking out his intonga sticks. "And you can't make us."

The men laugh so their bellies shake.

"You're very good at intonga, Tola," says Zoli, tapping his side. "But do you really think wood is a match for speeding metal?"

The boys notice a holster housing a pistol.

"Move!" Zoli insists.

The men haven't noticed the hole which is located a few feet to their right. Tola has to figure out a way to throw the vine in the hole without the men realizing what he did. He knows that Zoli would never shoot him given that Jogba has big plans for him. He whispers, "get the vine to Tata" but as he charges at Zoli he lets out a warlike yell.

Thabo hears the whole exchange between Tola and Zoli. His son is wise and brave beyond his years and Thabo is proud of him. His concern is for the safety of the boys. It doesn't sound like the men intend on using their guns except to scare the boys. He heard Zoli ask about a vine so he knows that the boys located one. How are they going to get it to him? Thabo continues to try to get a foothold somewhere to lift himself out.

Tola strikes Zoli's wrist and knocks the flashlight out of his hand. Then he smashes the flashlight and kicks it into the jungle while Zoli hollers in pain. Goatee-man grabs Tola and throws him down on the ground. Dumi and Vincent dash to the hole and lower the vine down to Thabo. Then they rush the men to assist their friend.

"Stop!" Zoli roars, taking out his gun.

The boys freeze.

"Get up!" says Zoli, grabbing Tola's shirt and yanking him to his feet. "Walk."

Zoli pushes Tola forward. He gives Vincent and Dumi a look that lets them know that they are expected to follow. They don't walk far.

Thabo scrambles up the rope. He sees the two men leading the boys to the compound. He clutches his intonga rod and creeps up behind Zoli. He swiftly strikes the hand holding the gun and in the same motion smacks his Adam's apple. Zoli clutches his throat as he falls to the ground gasping. Thabo picks up the gun and points it at the goatee-man who puts up his hands.

"Get on your knees," Thabo orders.

The man complies.

"Are you boys alright?" Thabo asks.

"We are fine, Tata," says Tola, embracing his dad. His friends concur. "How about you? Is anything broken?"

Thabo laughs. "It'll take a lot more than a short fall to break me, young man. I'm not that old."

Tola smiles though he is a little concerned. Tata was knocked unconscious and could have a concussion. One of his teammates got a concussion playing soccer and it was so serious that he was taken off the team for this year. Tola says a silent prayer for his dad.

Thabo uses the same vine that rescued him to tie up Zoli and the goatee-man. He binds their hands behind them, fastens their legs together, then secures them to separate trees. Then he throws the gun into the hole that he fell into.

"Let's go," says Thabo.

"Are we going to rescue our teammates?" asks Tola.

"We are, but not yet. We have to wait for reinforcements. They might be at the meeting spot already. We have to hurry."

"Wait," says Tola. "This belongs to you."

He hands Tata the rod with the names of his sisters.

"I found this and when I saw the names, I realized that it was you chasing us. That's why we came back looking for you."

"Then it's a good thing I dropped it, isn't it, son?"

"It's a God thing, Tata."

"That's right, my son."

Thabo hugs Tola and kisses his head. With one backward look to ensure the prisoners are still bound, Thabo leads the boys to the meeting spot.

Chapter 13

"We should be going home," says Thabo.

They have been sitting for about ten minutes engaging in small talk. Thabo is concerned that someone will notice that Zoli and his cohort are missing and might search for them.

"Not without our teammates, Tata," says Tola.

Thabo takes a deep breath. It could be another hour before the officers return with the cavalry. The camp is still and it looks like everyone has turned in for the night. But all they have are sticks which are no match for guns. It will be foolhardy to place all their lives at risk and mount some sort of rescue.

"We'll wait a little longer," Thabo says. He looks at Tola's friends. "How are you boys holding up."

"We are fine, Mr. Matthews," says Victor. Dumi nods in agreement.

The tremor in his voice is not lost on Thabo. He glances at Tola whose facial expression shows that he noticed it too.

Thabo smiles. "The officers will be here soon. Don't worry. You'll be back in your beds tonight."

They had better come soon, Thabo thinks.

It is a few minutes later that a bearded man steps out of his hut and looks around. He calls out the names of 'Zoli' and 'Chuks'.

"Stay down," says Thabo.

The man continues to look around and call out the names. He disappears into some dwellings and reappears looking puzzled or annoyed.

Tola looks up and peers through some bushes.

"He's eventually going to go to our area," he says. "He might notice that we're missing."

"Let's hope not," says Thabo. "Where are those guys?"

Thabo is exasperated. The situation is getting precarious.

"We have to go, boys," says Thabo. "It's too risky. The police are on their way. They will take care of your friends."

As he spoke, Zoli and Chuks dashed into view, yelling something they couldn't make out.

"They managed to untie themselves," says Dumi, stating the obvious.

They huddle with the bearded man and then look out into the jungle. Chuks dives into a hut and comes out with a powerful flashlight that he points around the perimeter.

Thabo puts his finger to his lips and gestures for everyone to lay low. The light sweeps past them and then returns as Chuks does another sweep. Chuks turns off the light and Thabo sees them in another huddle. Then the three men stride into Chuks' hut.

"Let's go," whispers Thabo.

They get up and slowly move out. They have barely made five steps when Chuks shines a light on them.

"Stop!" Chuks yells.

Thabo doesn't hesitate. There is no way his son is going back to being kidnapped by these thugs.

"Run, boys!" he bellows.

Chapter 14

Tola, Vincent, and Dumi follow after Thabo as he seeks trees with luminescent paint.

"This way," Thabo says.

Thankfully, the luminescence is easy to follow so they can run without being slowed down by which way to go. They have enough hindrances with the jungle. Thabo is pleased to see that the boys are keeping up.

"Keep running," he encourages.

A gunshot rings out. They hear the bullet rustle through leaves and thump into a tree.

"Go ahead of me," Thabo says, allowing Tola to lead. "Follow the yellow paint."

Tola knows what his dad means. They had used similar techniques on adventures back in Dlambona. Commonly they would stab a milk tree and let the white sap run. Even when dry, the residue is visible at night. Tola has his head on a swivel looking for the yellow marker and seeking the best path to take.

Another shot rings out. The bang from the gun is closer.

"I can't run much more," says Dumi.

"Come on, Dumi," says Tola. "We've run further than this. They're getting closer."

They take a few more steps before Dumi stumbles and falls. Tola and Vincent grab him and force him to continue but he staggers to the ground.

Another shot rings out. This time even closer.

"They must have seen the yellow paint," says Thabo. "You fellows go on ahead. I'm going to lead them away from you."

With all that had happened to him today, he still had the small spray can of yellow paint.

"No, Tata," says Tola. "We should stick together."

"We don't have time to discuss this, Tola," says Thabo. "Go!"

Thabo sprays the nearest tree and continues spraying ensuring that the chasers see it and follows him and is misdirected from the boys. He is so focused on it that he is startled by Tola coming up behind him.

"Tola, what are you doing? Where are your friends?"

"They will be fine, Tata. I believe your plan is going to work so they'll be safe. I told them to find a place to hide."

The plan does work as the pursuers turn to hunt them down.

"Tola, when this is over, you and I are going to have a conversation. Keep up."

Tola smiles as he vaults a small bush. If he and Tata are going to have a conversation, it means that they will get home safe and sound. Thabo sprays a final tree and they continue their getaway.

"It's no use giving them any more breadcrumbs," says Thabo.

The pursuers wouldn't need signs. Thabo and Tola suddenly break through the jungle and stumble onto a small clearing. Without the canopy of the jungle, the moonlight illuminates the area. Zoli and company will have no problem picking them off if they found them in the open space. But that is not the immediate problem. With rifles pointed at them stood two boys that Thabo recognized.

"Thomas and Sipho, let us proceed please," implores Thabo

"You're not going anywhere," says Sipho.

Chapter 15

Zoli, Chuks, and the bearded man appear on the scene. Thabo moves Tola behind him as he attempts to shield his son from what might come.

"Well done, young men," Zoli says, showing Sipho and Thomas his approval. He looks at Tola and shakes his head in disgust. "Tola, why are you taking advantage of our goodwill? We treated you with respect and wanted you to lead our soldiers. Look at where your actions have led us."

Thabo continues to try to shield Tola. Chuks approaches to try and pull Tola away from him but all he gets is Thabo's right cross to his face.

"I don't think so," says Zoli, pointing his gun at Thabo, who puts his hands up. Zoli eyes Sipho and Thomas and gestures to Tola with his head. "Get him!"

"Let my Tata go," says Tola, brandishing his intonga sticks. "It's me you want."

"I have a gun, you fool," says Zoli. He laughs. "Jogba is right. You are like a wild horse that needs to be broken."

He approaches Tola and it is all Tola could do to not strike him with his sticks.

"And break you we will," says Zoli. "It will be best for you if you cooperate. Take Tola back to camp. I will follow after I have dealt with the father."

Zoli pulls the sticks from Tola's grasp and pushes him to the ground. Chuks, Sipho, and Thomas grab him and lift him and drag him away. Tola is not going easily and flails his body, dragging his feet and becoming limp.

"Leave him alone!" says Thabo and rushes to assist his son.

Zoli strikes him across the shins with the sticks and Thabo falls, groaning at the pain.

"Where do you think you're going?" asks Zoli, standing over Thabo as he writhes in pain.

"We could ask you the same thing," says Officer Kamau, as he appears out of the jungle.

He is not alone. Five other officers flank him, guns are drawn and they relieve Zoli and his cronies of their weapons. Tola runs to his Tata and they embrace.

"Can we join in?" asks Vincent.

He and Dumi come behind the police and join the happy reunion.

"We ran into these fellows and they told us what happened," says Kamau. "Finding you wasn't difficult with that paint of yours, Thabo. It was a good idea."

"Well, we're glad you got here when you did," says Thabo. "We still have to rescue the other boys. Let's go."

"Easy, my friend," says Kamau. "The army raided the camp and rescued everyone there. Your teammates are safe."

The boys high-fived each other.

"We have a bit of a distance to walk to the buses," says Kamau. "Are you all up for it?"

"Of course we are," responds Dumi. "We've been running all night and could run another night without difficulty. Let's go."

Tola and Vincent share a glance and shake their heads. Then Tola puts his hand in his dad's and squeezes. As they walk he looks up and gives Jesus thanks for never leaving nor forsaking them.

Epilogue

Tola, Vincent, Dumi, and the football team are allowed to take a few days off before returning to school. Tola decides to take one day off. He uses that day to recuperate from his adventure.

When he wakes up at noon, he is met by the aroma of beef stew, dumplings, and rice. Mama knows just what a son needs. He showers and then joins the family for lunch. As they enjoy their meal, Officer Kamau shows up.

"Will you please join us, Kamau?" says Jalisa. "There is plenty to eat."

"Thank you, Jalisa, but I have just eaten. I'll have a glass of water if I can, please."

"Of course," says Jalisa. "Tola, get the officer some water, please."

Kamau had a sombre look on his face. Everyone notices and waits for him to provide whatever news he had. Kamau takes a sip of his water.

"Jogba escaped," he says.

"What," says Jalisa. "What happened?"

"We're guessing that when his men chased after Thabo and the boys, he correctly thought that the police must be close and made a run for it."

"Did you find their trucks?" asks Tola. "We had to walk pretty far to the camp after getting out of the vehicles."

"We did. They hid them well but we were able to locate two pick-up trucks."

"And a Peugeot 504," says Tola.

"No," says Kamau. "Just the trucks."

"Jogba must have driven off in the Peugeot," says Tola, crestfallen. "I was hoping that I didn't have to worry about seeing that car again."

He finishes his lunch and asks to be excused. Lindi asks him if he can take her to the playground. As he pushes her on the swing, he thinks about his ordeal and ponders what it might be like going back to school tomorrow. It's going to be difficult for many of his teammates. He feels that some won't return to the football team which would be understandable.

"Push me higher," says Lindi, gleefully.

Life must go on. He grabs the swing seat and sprints forward, lifting it high as he runs underneath it. Lindi shrieks in delight.

Tola repeats.